Peterkin
Meets a Star

Emilie Boon

CORGI BOOKS
A DIVISION OF TRANSWORLD PUBLISHERS LTD.

Peterkin went for an evening walk.

He saw a bright star shining.

Peterkin reached for it.

He carried it home

and fell asleep holding it.

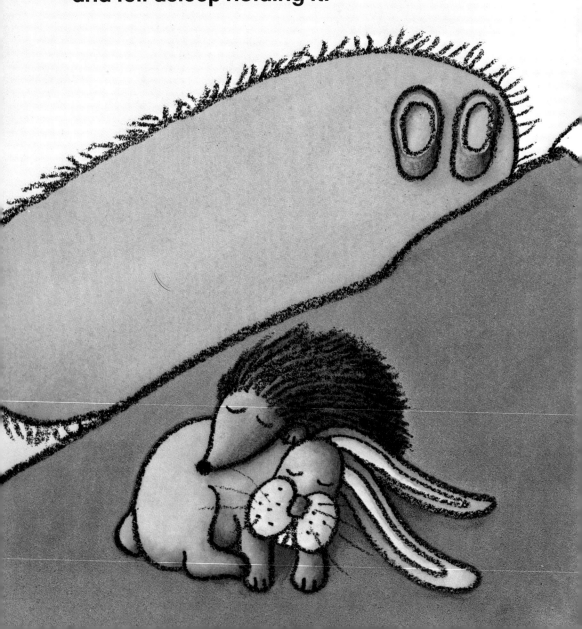

Next morning the star looked dim.

It wouldn't eat breakfast.

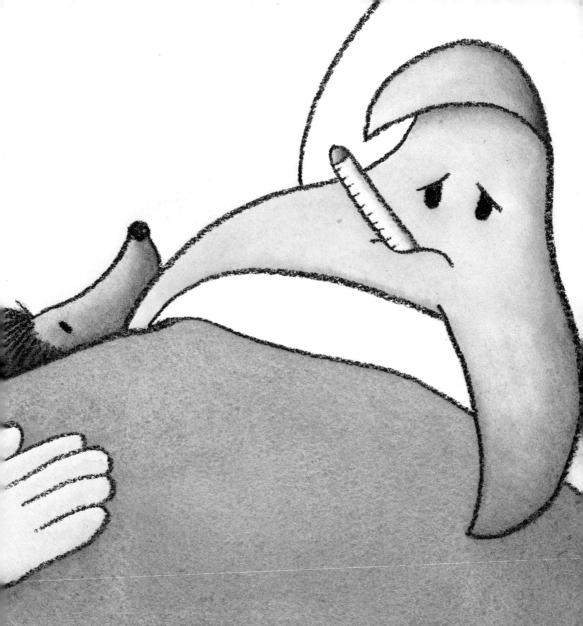

Peterkin tucked it into bed.

At dusk he took it out for some air.

The star began to twinkle again.

So Peterkin put it back in the sky

and waved goodbye

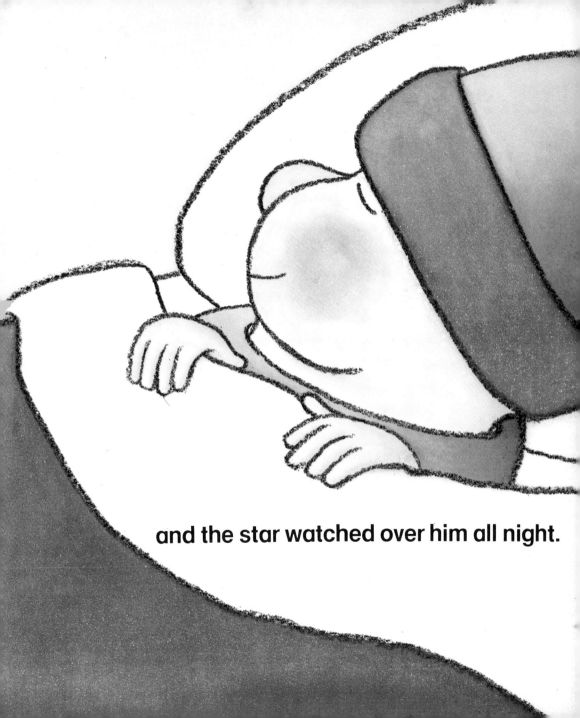

and the star watched over him all night.